CRABTREE SCHOOL

Year Two
Forever and Ever

Lauren Pearson
Illustrated by Becka Moor

■SCHOLASTIC

For the real Ava and Johnny,
and their dad

Chapter

Breakfast Is the Most
Important Meal of the Day

The first day of school can be the best day and it can be the worst day.

Ava Alexandra Hughes, who was seven years old, was thinking about this while she waited for her Weetabix to get soggy. Weetabix taste much better when they are soggy, and even better still once you've used your spoon to shape them into a castle or a tree or an animal. Weetabix sculptures are delicious.

It was the morning of Ava's first day of Year Three at Crabtree School for Girls. Crabtree School was quite simply the best primary

1

school in all of Great Britain, and probably the world. It had the kindest teachers, the cleverest students, and the best playground of any school, anywhere. Everyone said so. Girls came from miles around to go there, but luckily for Ava it was right at the end of her street. Being only a short walk away from the school was especially good because eating breakfast at Ava's house tended to take a long time.

Across the table, Ava's little brother was eating his Rice Krispies one by one. Johnny was four years old and he would never, ever eat Weetabix, soggy or crispy. Not since the terrible time he'd spread them all over the bottom of his bare feet. He did this because the Weetabix felt nice and squishy. But then squishy turned to sticky, and whilst Johnny stood at the sink washing the Weetabix off his *hands*, the Weetabix on his *feet* dried like cement. It took Ava dumping a whole pint of milk over Johnny's

feet to unstick him. Mum had not been happy.

Ava watched as Johnny dipped his fork into his apple juice. He wasn't the usual sort of naughty little brother that you always hear about. He tried so hard to be good, but most of the time it just didn't work out that way. (In fact, it almost never worked out that way.)

Today was Johnny's first day of school too. He was going to be in Reception at Dogwood School for Boys. Ava worried about what school would be like for Johnny without her there to watch out for him and pour milk on his toes. But Johnny didn't seem scared. And anyway, if you asked Ava, Reception wasn't like school at all. It was more like being at a soft play centre, with breaks for stories and snacks. Not nearly as serious as Year Three was going to be. Year Three was big time.

"Johnny!" Mum interrupted Ava's thoughts. "Stop trying to drink your juice with a fork!

Come on, you two, eat everything all up!"

Ava slowly chewed a bite of Weetabix and went back to thinking about first days of school. Three years ago on her *own* first day of Reception at Crabtree School, Ava's class sat down to lunch in the big school dining room. Or rather everyone else sat down. Ava fell down. She missed her chair and landed flat on her bum on the floor. She knocked the table as she went and then her jacket potato fell too. It landed on her head. There were baked beans and cheese dripping down her face, right in front of everyone. The teachers were watching. The older girls were watching. Her new classmates were watching. It was the worst thing that could possibly happen to you on your first day of Reception. Ava was so embarrassed she couldn't move.

Then came an amazing moment: a girl in Ava's class, Zoe, stood up from the table.

She picked up her lunch and she sat down on the dining room floor next to Ava. Zoe smiled at Ava. They both giggled. Then another Reception girl called Lottie brought her potato down too, and joined them under the table. So did a third girl, called Isabel. One by one, each of the Reception girls followed. They were all laughing, so Ava laughed too. She laughed so hard that she cried, while she picked beans out of her hair. Their entire Reception class had a jacket potato party on the floor. The rest of the school watched in amazement.

From then on everyone said that there was really something quite special about their year. The girls in Ava's class stuck together like a mixture of glue, syrup and honey.

Mum interrupted Ava's remembering again. "Finish your breakfast, I mean it now! We'll be late for school." The Weetabix were nice and mushy, and Ava had made them into a lovely bird. She took a bite of the Weetabix bird's tail.

"Ava," Mum went on, "have you seen the letter from Johnny's school? It was right here on the table and now it's gone."

"I haven't touched it," Ava replied.

Ava and Mum both looked at Johnny.

"Johnny," Mum said. "Have you seen Mummy's letter? It says what we need to bring for your first day of school. I want to check we have it all."

Johnny nodded yes. He was chewing on something. He knew better than to talk with his mouth full so Mum and Ava waited for him to finish. Mum tapped her foot and looked at her watch.

"Johnny," she said when he had swallowed. "Where is the letter?"

Ava noticed that there were bits of chewed-up typed words around Johnny's mouth. He smiled and then Ava saw that a tiny scrap of paper stuck across his top teeth read: PE KIT.

Johnny had eaten the letter.

Mum *had* said to eat up everything.

"Right," sighed Mum, handing Johnny his cup of juice. "Wash it down. We're off to school!"

So Ava didn't have any more time that morning to think about her first day of Year Three. But someone who could see into the future (which Ava couldn't) would have known that today was going to be the craziest, strangest, most totally unbelievable first day in the history of Crabtree School for Girls.

Chapter

Year Three, Here We Come

When Ava saw the huge red brick building with the rows of crab trees in front, she raced ahead of Johnny and her mum. It might seem strange to be excited that a long summer full of adventures was over, but Crabtree School for Girls was not just any school.

Crabtree School was on Crabtree Lane opposite Crabtree Park. Sometimes schools are named after roads or neighbourhoods, but in this case it was the school that came first. No one could remember what the road or the land was called before there was a school there. Crabtree School had been around for hundreds and hundreds of years.

There was something very special about this lovely old building filled with clever, happy, kind little girls. Whatever that something special was, it spread through the whole neighbourhood. No one could pass by without feeling just a little bit good inside. It was almost like Crabtree School was enchanted, except that it wasn't. The magic in this school was the kind that comes from real people and not from fairies, wizards or magicians.

Ava waved goodbye to Mum and Johnny, and made her way through the gates and up the path. She stepped carefully on to the slick polished floor of the school's front hallway. One of the most important rules at Crabtree School was NEVER to run on this bit of marble floor. It was so slippery that it was like an ice rink, especially when it was wet.

What was more, the office of the headmistress was right by the school's front door, and if you walked slowly enough, you might get invited in. Mrs Peabody almost always had her office door open, and if she saw a girl passing through the front hallway, the headmistress might offer her a cup of hot chocolate and a biscuit. Mrs Peabody was a headmistress of legendary kindness.

"Good morning, Ava," said Mrs Peabody

brightly. The headmistress was stood outside her office welcoming all of the girls, just as she was every morning when school was in session. Mrs Peabody was wearing a dress with very bright green and red flowers on it. It matched the colour of the crab apples on the trees outside. Mrs Peabody had fluffy hair that looked a bit like grey candyfloss.

"I hope you had a lovely summer," she said to Ava. "Miss Moody is upstairs waiting for you. She is most excited to be teaching your class this year!"

After saying hello to Mrs Peabody, Ava turned to look at the other lady who was always in the front hallway of Crabtree School. She wasn't nearly as cuddly as Mrs Peabody. This was because she was made of stone.

Standing at the foot of the school's big, winding staircase was a statue of Lady Constance Hawthorne. Lady Hawthorne was the very first headmistress of Crabtree School for Girls. Next to Lady Hawthorne's pointy, old-fashioned boots stood her little stone dog. He was called Baron Biscuit. Stroking him was meant to bring you good luck. Baron Biscuit had been stroked so many times by so many hands that his back was wearing away. These days he looked less like a dog and more like a camel with short legs.

Every morning of last year, a Year Six girl called Jessica would wait for Ava right here next to Baron Biscuit. Jessica was Ava's most grown-up friend. She always asked how Ava was and gave her a good-morning hug. Then Ava would watch Jessica go where all the big girls went: up the massive staircase to the first floor. The classrooms for years Three, Four, Five and Six were the only rooms upstairs, so Ava had never had a reason to go there.

Until today.

Ava knew that Jessica was long gone now, off to senior school. Ava missed her already. But to be finally climbing up those stairs herself felt like being invited into Santa's workshop. Ava practically floated to the first floor.

Miss Moody was standing at the Year Three classroom door with a big smile on her face. She looked like she was in a very good mood. Ava was relieved. Miss Moody is not a good name for a teacher. (Although it wasn't as bad as Miss Cross. She taught Year Four.)

In fact, Miss Moody was actually quite nervous about meeting her new Year Three class. Ever since that first day of Reception, word had got round about this group of girls.

You never knew what they would get up to next. Earlier that morning the Year Two teacher, who was called Miss Cheeky, had told Miss Moody to get ready; this Year Three was going to be one to remember.

Inside the Year Three classroom, there was wild chattering. It had been a long summer and there was lots to catch up on.

To Ava's delight, being in Year Three meant no more tables. Each girl had her own desk, with space inside to keep her things. You even got to choose which desk was yours. The chairs were bigger, the whiteboard was whiter and the view was better. From the high classroom windows you could see right out over Crabtree Park. Ava was extremely good at daydreaming and this looked like the perfect spot for it.

On this very morning, the park was full of mums and dads and children heading to other first days at other schools. There was also a woman without any children walking a huge dog. Maybe the woman was taking the dog to his first day of dog school...

"Ava!" called Zoe. "Ava, can you hear me? Sit here, next to me. Stop daydreaming and get that desk!"

The desk that Zoe was pointing to had Zoe on one side and the window on the other. It was perfect. Ava began to put her things away.

Zoe Eloise Ahlberg was Ava's best friend. During the jacket potato incident, Zoe had been the first one in their Reception class to sit down next to Ava on the floor. Now Zoe was seven years, six months and three days old. Zoe liked to keep an exact count of her age. Like Ava, Zoe had brown eyes, but Ava was tall with messy blondish hair that looked a bit like a bird's nest. Zoe was shorter – fifteen centimetres shorter, last they measured – with curly brown hair. Zoe always wore six hair clips, three on each side of her head, so her hair was never, ever messy.

Right then Zoe was counting out five pencils and arranging them neatly inside her desk. Zoe had a separate pencil for every day of the week. She also always wore two watches, one on each wrist.

"Ava, it has been fifty-seven days since we have last been in school. And twelve days since our last play date." Zoe loved numbers. A LOT. Ava liked to say that Zoe wanted to marry numbers.

"Where did you have your play date?" called a voice from the back of the room. Charlotte Christina Lewis was seven years old, too. Only her grans called her Charlotte, everyone else called her Lottie. Except her cousins, who called her Charlie. And her Dad, who called her Doodles. Lottie liked having lots of different names. It made it harder for people to keep track of her.

Lottie had chin-length brown hair and huge brown eyes that were always looking about for things to watch. When she wore her glasses, her eyes looked even bigger. Lottie liked to know everything that was happening to everybody all the time. Whatever she found out, she wrote down in the purple notebook that she always carried with her. That way she could remember it forever.

Lottie had chosen a desk in the back by the window. From there she could keep one eye on the classroom and the other eye on the school gates and the park. If Lottie could have got away with it, she would have drilled a little hole in the floor so that she could spy on the class below too.

"The play date was at my house," Ava told Lottie, and Lottie wrote that down in her notebook. Lottie had filled so many purple notebooks since Reception that Ava thought she must have a whole room at home with used notebooks stacked to the ceiling. It must be a secret room too, because Ava had been to Lottie's house loads of times and had never seen it.

Lottie came round to Ava's desk and was filling in details on the play date from twelve days ago.

Ava watched Lottie fill in the entry. Usually play dates weren't top secret, unless you had an argument or did something really naughty.

"Isabel came to that play date too," said Ava helpfully, pointing at Lottie's notebook page. Lottie added Isabel's name.

Isabel Elizabeth Donaldson was eight years old, which is a huge difference from being seven. She had blonde hair that was always in two straight plaits, and freckles arranged neatly across her nose. Isabel was quite tall, and she always stood very straight.

Isabel had also got down on the floor with Ava on that first day of Reception. That was really something, because Isabel was the best-behaved girl in their whole class. This could have made her boring, but it didn't.

That morning, Isabel had chosen a desk in the front row, right opposite Miss Moody's. She was sitting there now with her hands folded. She kept turning around to listen to Zoe, Ava and Lottie, but she didn't get out of her seat. Isabel wanted to make a good first impression on Miss Moody.

"Isabel had loads of play dates over the summer," said Lottie, flipping through her notebook. Ava knew that was because Isabel liked to get away from her little twin sisters.

Just then Miss Moody came into the classroom, still in a good mood. "Girls," she said. "Welcome to my class! I have heard so much about you all. And I can't wait to tell you all of the wonderful things we are going to get up to! But first let me ask you: what do you know about Year Three?"

Ava's class knew a lot about Year Three. Zoe knew that Year Three meant that you were no longer in the youngest half of the school. In Year Three, you were precisely in the middle. Isabel knew it meant swimming lessons in the spring term, and someone else knew about the overnight camping trip during summer term. Lottie, of course, knew *everything* about Year Three, even more than Miss Moody, but she didn't raise her hand because she was too busy writing down what everyone was saying.

"Wow, girls!" Miss Moody exclaimed. "You've heard a lot about Year Three! There's even more to come, but right now we've got an assembly for the whole school. Line up, please!"

Chapter

Um

Ava's class made their way down the stairs towards the assembly room. They passed the big school kitchen, where they could smell apple crumble baking in the oven. Next, Year Three walked past the very best room in the school. It was called the Rainbow Room because it was bright and happy in there even when it was raining and horrible outside. The door to the Rainbow Room was open. Ava could see the fairy lights on the ceiling. There was also a soft fuzzy rug and bean bag chairs. The Rainbow Room was used for special activities, like drama lessons and famous authors who came to visit. It was also a great place for watching films. In the corner was a real-life, old-fashioned popcorn maker, just like you see at a funfair.

Ava loved going to the Rainbow Room. Everyone did. Lottie kept a whole list in her notebook called **TIMES WE HAVE BEEN TO THE RAINBOW ROOM**. The older you got, the more chances there were for being in the Rainbow Room, so Ava was hoping that Lottie's list would get very long in Year Three, and that there would be lots of popcorn.

As her class filed into the assembly room, Ava saw that the new Reception girls, who were having their first EVER first day of school, were looking very scared. Everyone else was happy to be back.

Mrs Peabody stepped up on the stage. She smoothed her lovely dress and patted her fluffy hair. She smiled a special smile that she kept for first days of school. "Girls, I am delighted to welcome you back," she said. "I missed all of you so much over the summer." She looked round at them, taking time to smile at each and every girl.

But when she got to the back of the room, she stopped smiling.

Mrs Peabody squinted her eyes. She smooshed her lips to one side, then the other.

Then she frowned.

Mrs Peabody did not frown very often.

"Um," she said.

Something was wrong. Headmistresses do not say "um". Headmistresses are the ones who tell YOU not to say "um".

"Um," Mrs Peabody went on. She was looking at something in the back of the room. "Um ... um..."

The entire school twisted round to see what it was.

There, standing in the assembly room door, was a truly spectacular sight: it was Jessica! Ava wanted to jump up and hug her tall, grown-up, eleven-year-old friend with the messy fringe and twinkling blue eyes.

But wait. What was Jessica still doing at Crabtree School? In her Crabtree School uniform? Jessica didn't go to Crabtree School any more. Jessica was in Year Seven. Crabtree School did not have a Year Seven.

At first Ava thought she must be daydreaming. But other people can't see your daydreams and Mrs Peabody could definitely see Jessica. So could Isabel: her eyes looked like they were going to pop out of her head. In fact, everyone in the school was now staring at the back of the assembly room.

(Everyone except the new Reception class, that is. The new Reception class were staring at their shoes and trying not to cry.)

"What are they doing here?" whispered Zoe to Ava. "It's all twenty-four of them!"

Ava had been so focused on Jessica that she hadn't noticed that Jessica wasn't alone. Next to Jessica was Elizabeth, another of last year's leavers. She was whispering in Jessica's ear. That didn't surprise Ava because Elizabeth never stopped talking. And there was Lucy who wore sparkly headbands, and Diya who could do twelve cartwheels and ... in fact there was the whole of the Year Six class from last year. They were spread out along the back wall of the assembly room.

"Um," said Mrs Peabody, again. Then she

called Mrs Swan, the Year Six teacher, over to the stage. They did some whispering. And some head-shaking. It was clear that Mrs Swan had no idea what last year's leavers were doing in assembly. Mrs Peabody tried a few other teachers. No one knew anything.

"Um," Mrs Peabody said again, looking round the room. "Charlotte Lewis? Lottie? Where are you, darling? Come to the stage, please."

Mrs Peabody knew that if there was anyone in the whole school who might know what Jessica's class was doing there, it was Lottie. But for once Lottie didn't know anything either.

Mrs Peabody had no choice but to muddle through. "Good morning, um, Crabtree girls," she said, again. "As I said, lovely to have you back. All of you. Um…" Ava noticed that Zoe was counting on her fingers the number of times the headmistress said "um". She was running out of fingers, but Mrs Peabody kept going.

"Especially all of you from last year's Year Six class, I'm so glad you came to visit. And in your old uniforms too. Um, how lovely. Just lovely. So lovely to see you. Really, really lovely." Now Zoe was counting "lovely"s. Ava had never heard Mrs Peabody blabber on like this before. Luckily, Jessica put her hand up.

"Yes, Jessica?" Mrs Peabody looked relieved that someone else was going to talk for a minute.

"Mrs Peabody, we aren't visiting," said Jessica. "We've decided to come back to Crabtree. We want to stay here."

"All day?" asked Mrs Peabody.

"No," said Jessica. "For forever and ever."

The assembly room went very, very quiet.

"I don't understand," said Mrs Peabody. "What about your new schools? What about Year Seven?"

"We aren't going to our new schools," said Jessica's classmate Elizabeth. "Not now and not ever. Never, never, never." Once Elizabeth started talking there was no stopping her. "We are staying in Year Six. For forever and ever and ever and ever. Like Jessica said. All of us. Me, Jessica, Lucy, Harriet, Olivia, Talia—"

She would have named the whole class but Mrs Peabody interrupted her. "Now girls," said the headmistress, "you can't possibly—"

"But you can't be in Year Six," screeched one of the *new* Year Six girls. "WE are Year Six now! We can't have TWO Year Sixes!" She hadn't raised her hand but Mrs Peabody didn't seem to notice.

"Yes," called out someone else. "And WE are Year Five!"

"Year Five, Year Five!" The new Year Fives began chanting.

Suddenly there was the sound of crying. A LOT of crying. The new Reception class were sobbing as loud as ten thousand babies without their dummies. All this screeching and shouting had scared them.

Ava didn't blame them for crying. She had been waiting for YEARS to be in Year Three. Spending forever and ever in Year Two – without your own desk, without swimming, without a real life sleepover class trip with all of your friends – didn't sound at all brilliant. It sounded horribly, terribly, awfully bad.

Chapter

4

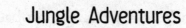

Jungle Adventures

It was a well-known fact at Crabtree School that Mrs Peabody simply could not bear the sound of a child crying. The very *idea* of crying made the headmistress's knees knock, her legs wobble, her arms shake and her hair stand on end. This fear of tears was one of the things that made Mrs Peabody a headmistress of such legendary kindness. That morning, it also made her completely useless. When she saw an entire Reception class of twenty-four four-year-olds weeping and wailing, Mrs Peabody panicked.

She ordered *last year's* Year Six class back to the Year Six classroom like naughty children being sent to their bedrooms. But then she had nothing to do with the *new* Year Six class. So she told them to go to Year Five. Then she told the new Year Five class to go back to Year Four. And so on. There were so many unhappy Crabtree girls stomping around the assembly room that the crab apples on the trees outside began to shake.

"All of you, collect your things and go back to wherever you were last year!" Mrs Peabody cried. "Please! Just until we get this sorted!" She sent the new Reception class to the Rainbow Room with Mrs Crunch. Mrs Crunch was the school dinner lady. She was very kind and always smelled like apple crumble. If anyone could stop the Reception girls crying, it was Mrs Crunch.

"Jessica and Elizabeth," Mrs Peabody shouted

over the noise, "as soon as the room clears, I want you in my office!" It didn't sound like biscuits and hot chocolate would be on offer.

As Year Three, which was now Year Two again, filed out of the assembly room, Lottie hovered in the hallway. "We've got to find out what's going on," she told Ava and Zoe. She pointed at the door to Mrs Peabody's office. It was open just a little bit. "I've got to get in there, so I can hear what they say to Mrs Peabody!"

"No way!" said Isabel. "Sneaking into the headmistress's office? That is the naughtiest thing you could ever possibly do!"

"Surely not," said Ava, thinking out loud. "It would be much naughtier to take a big tray of Mrs Crunch's apple crumble and tip it out all over Mrs Peabody's car..."

The other girls looked at Ava. That did sound very *naughty*, but hiding in the headmistress's office was *sneaky*. Grown-ups really don't like sneaky, even when it is for their own good.

"We have no choice," said Zoe. "If the Year Sixes don't leave, they'll clog up the whole school. We'll be stuck in Year Two, and within five years Crabtree will have, let's see. . ." Zoe did a bit of maths. "*More than one hundred* Reception girls!"

Everyone gasped.

"This could ruin Crabtree School," said Lottie. Ava had to agree. There would be Crabtree girls all over the place; they'd be wedged in the building like crayons in a box. They'd be popping out of the windows and hanging from the ceilings.

"Every year," said Zoe, "there is the perfect number of five-year-olds and the perfect number of eleven-year-olds and the perfect number of everyone in between. And it has to stay that way."

Zoe was right again. Ava pictured a huge crowd of grandmothers, mothers, big sisters and children all turning up for assembly together in their Crabtree uniforms. It would be beyond silly. Crabtree School just wouldn't be the same.

"I'm doing it!" Lottie decided. She slid her notebook into her dress pocket and pulled up her socks. Then in a flash she disappeared behind the heavy door that read: MRS PEABODY.

As her class headed upstairs to get their things, Ava thought that even Baron Biscuit looked shocked at what Lottie had done. Ava stroked his back for the second time that day. They needed all the luck they could get.

Miss Moody did not notice that Lottie was missing as she led the class, who were now carrying their coats and pencil cases, back down to the Year Two classroom. It was horrible; Ava looked back at the stairs sadly and tried not to cry. She felt like a baby being led back to nursery.

Once they got to Year Two, Miss Cheeky, who had been their teacher last year and was now their teacher again, *did* notice that Lottie was missing. But Miss Cheeky had a whole year of experience with this class. She was used to Lottie disappearing all the time. She knew that Lottie would come back once her mission was over.

The girls sat down at the tables that now felt too small. They'd been fine last year, but their class had obviously done loads of growing over the summer.

Ava stared out into the car park. It was a terrible view for inspiring daydreams. She missed Year Three already.

The rest of the class stared at Miss Cheeky. Miss Cheeky stared back at them. Nobody knew what to do. "Welcome to Year Two," she finally said. "Again!"

Lottie hadn't come back. Maybe she had already been found out. Maybe at this very moment Mrs Peabody was on the phone to Lottie's mum. Ava couldn't stand it any longer.

"Miss Cheeky, please may I go to the toilet?"

Zoe wasn't about to miss out. "Me too, please, Miss Cheeky?"

Miss Cheeky couldn't be bothered to make them go one at a time. Plus she guessed they were off to find Lottie, which wouldn't be a bad thing.

"Be quick, girls!" she said. "And please don't talk in the hallway. It's noisy enough around here with all the new Reception girls crying."

Zoe and Ava didn't speak as they walked down the hall. Sometimes best friends don't need words. They nodded and pointed their way into the kitchen, sneaked out of the side door and tiptoed down the pebble path that wound round the side of the school. They crouched beneath the window of Mrs Peabody's office, hidden in the crab trees.

"If we get caught out here, we'll be in bigger trouble than Lottie," said Zoe. It was against the rules to be out in front of the school on your own during the day.

Together they peered into Mrs Peabody's window. There was no sign of Lottie. Mrs Peabody sat in her big chair. The school cat, Lady Lovelypaws, was asleep in a tray on her desk. Jessica and Elizabeth were in smaller chairs opposite the headmistress. Everyone was looking very serious. Ava and Zoe couldn't hear a word they were saying.

Luckily, Mrs Peabody couldn't hear anything outside either, because just then a crab apple fell right on Ava's head. She yelped. Lady

Lovelypaws raised her head and looked towards the window.

"SSSSSSSSSSHHHHHHHHHHHHHHH HHHHHHH!" hissed Zoe.

"Where is Lottie?" whispered Ava, rubbing her head. "She must be in there somewhere."

"She's very good at hiding," said Zoe. "Even if she's still in there we might never spot her."

Ava looked very, very carefully. The office was tidy and there weren't that many hiding places. There was Mrs Peabody's big desk, a coat stand, the two visitors' chairs and a huge potted plant in the corner. They could see that Lottie wasn't underneath any of the furniture, and even she couldn't hide behind a coat stand.

"Look!" whispered Zoe. "Look at the plant! It has shoes!"

The plant did indeed have shoes, right where the stem met the pot. If you looked very closely, it also had legs and a stripy dress. Lottie was

standing in the pot, hidden amongst the leaves. It was like she was in a very small jungle. Ava had to stare for a long time to see her, but once she had, she saw the plant rustle slightly, as if Lottie were moving around. Then her notebook appeared though the leaves. Written in big block letters were the words: HELP! NEED OUT! NEED A WEE!

"Attention, Miss Ahlberg. Attention, Miss Hughes!" a voice boomed from behind them. Ava and Zoe jumped like popcorn in the Rainbow Room popcorn-maker. They were not as good at spying as Lottie was. They had been caught by Colonel Crunch, the school groundskeeper. Colonel Crunch was married to Mrs Crunch. About a million years ago he had been a soldier in the army. Now he was in charge of all the building, gardening, fixing, planting, cleaning, organizing, mowing, weeding, light-bulb-changing and lost-scooter-finding at Crabtree School.

Colonel Crunch saluted Ava and Zoe. A thousand stories about why they were out there flashed through Ava's mind. But Zoe wisely decided that it was better to tell the truth. In less than a minute, she told Colonel Crunch the whole terrible tale about how last year's leavers wouldn't leave, how she and her friends only wanted to help and how brave Lottie had been. By the time she had finished the Colonel was bent down peeking in the window too. Now Lottie needed the loo so badly that she was hopping up and down, and the whole plant was shaking. Lady Lovelypaws was ready to pounce on it.

"Hundreds of Reception girls would be a lot to clean up after," Colonel Crunch said. "They would ruin my playground." Colonel Crunch kept the Crabtree School playground very tidy. He loved nothing more than a shiny slide and a bright, freshly painted climbing frame.

"So you'll help us?" asked Zoe. "We've got to get Lottie out."

"At your service," said Colonel Crunch. He marched off towards the school's front door.

"We've got to get back to Miss Cheeky," said Zoe to Ava. She looked at one of her watches. "We've been gone almost nine minutes."

"Look!" whispered Ava. Inside the office, Mrs Peabody, Jessica, Elizabeth and Lady Lovelypaws had all turned to look at the door. Colonel Crunch appeared with a huge trolley. He saluted Mrs Peabody and then he pointed to the plant. He picked it up, put it on the trolley and wheeled it out. He turned and saluted Mrs Peabody again, just as the bell for morning break time rang.

Ava and Zoe dashed back inside. Their class was already in the hallway, on their way out to the playground for break time. Ava and Zoe followed them, and when Colonel Crunch

passed by the queue with his trolley, Lottie jumped out and joined her friends. She had leaves in her hair.

"Wow!" Ava told her. "You did it!"

"Mission accomplished!" said Lottie proudly, stopping outside the door to the toilets. "But the report is terrible: Year Six are here to stay."

"For forever and ever?" asked Zoe.

"Maybe even longer," Lottie replied.

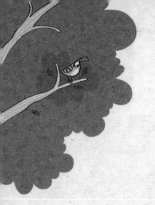

Chapter

An Idea Begins to Grow

The first disastrous day of school was over and Ava, Lottie and Zoe were at Isabel's house for a very special back-to-school play date. (This was play date number ninety-five in Lottie's notebook.) Their mums had come along too, and so had all the littlies: Lottie's younger sister Lola, and Isabel's little twin sisters, Scarlett and Ruby. Scarlett and Ruby (or the Reds, as Isabel called them) were three-and-a-half and naughtier than the naughtiest thing you can possibly think of. They drove Isabel bonkers.

There were two brothers at the play date

as well: Zoe's brother, Rafe, who was a baby really and just learning to walk, and of course Johnny. After a quick snack, the littlies went out to the garden and the big girls headed for Isabel's room.

Even though Isabel's sisters were annoying, Ava loved going to Isabel's house. She *especially* loved Isabel's room. Isabel was always doing crafts, and on any given day you might find a group of animals made out of socks having a tea party on Isabel's bed, or some potatoes with drawing-pin eyes giving a concert on a stage made out of a cereal box.

Isabel also had a huge collection of conkers that she had turned into little conker people. (She'd tried this with the crab apples from school too, but they tended to rot and get stinky.) There were little girl conkers with wool glued on for bunches and slightly bigger conkers that were mummies and daddies. There was

even a doctor conker, with a stethoscope made out of string and a button. Most of the conkers lived in a doll's house in the corner; a few more lived in the Barbie caravan.

Ava sat down on the floor and began sorting through the conkers to see if there were any new ones since she'd last been to Isabel's.

"What we need," said Zoe, "is a plan. A proper one." She was hanging upside down off the side of Isabel's bed. Being upside down helped her think.

For the third time that day, the girls made Lottie tell them about what she had heard in the headmistress's office. The reason that the Year Sixes wouldn't leave, Jessica had told Mrs Peabody, was because they loved Crabtree School so much. They had all got together over the summer and their whole class felt the same way: they loved the building, they loved the teachers, they loved the food, they loved Baron

Biscuit and Lady Lovelypaws, and they loved Mrs Peabody. No other school could possibly have the same magic.

Lottie said the headmistress had had a difficult time arguing with them, especially when they said they loved her.

"Didn't she tell them they HAD to leave?" asked Zoe. "That their new schools are waiting for them?"

"Yes," said Lottie, who was having a snoop through Isabel's drawers. "But then Jessica started crying because she loves Crabtree School so much. And you know what happens to Mrs Peabody when she sees crying."

They all nodded.

"I don't see why she can't just shove them out the door," said Zoe. "All of them, before they get the chance to cry." Zoe was going quite red in the face from being upside down. Ava thought she was beginning to look like a tomato, hanging there like that.

"Headmistresses can't go around shoving people," said Isabel. "But why didn't Mrs Peabody just call their mummies?"

"She did," said Lottie. "But it sounded like the mums were happy for them to stay. Mrs Peabody kept saying, 'Yes, Mrs Blah-Blah, they do grow up so very fast'."

"Ugh," said Zoe. "Mums never want you to grow up." Ava knew that Zoe said this because Zoe really, really wanted pierced ears and her mum said not until she was twenty-five.

"Anyway, Mrs Peabody said that she would ring their new schools and tell the heads that they will be coming soon," Lottie went on. "But then Jessica and Elizabeth said not to do that because they would never, ever be coming. They said if she even talked about them leaving again, they would cry for forever and ever."

"What did Mrs Peabody say then?" asked

Ava, smoothing the long hair on a conker that looked like Rapunzel.

"I don't know," said Lottie. "That's when Colonel Crunch came to rescue me."

Just then there was a loud rumbling sound from outside of Isabel's room. They could hear the littlies come bounding up the stairs like a herd of baby elephants.

"Oh no," cried Zoe, whose face had gone from tomato-red to more of a grape-purple. "Here they come!"

Before the littlies reached the top of the stairs, Isabel very calmly went and closed her bedroom door. Ava knew that Isabel was hoping against all hope that the littlies would go and play in her sisters' room.

"But I like having the old Year Sixes around," said Ava. "Maybe they could just stay?"

"As long as they are here we are all stuck," said Zoe. "We've already missed six hours and thirty-five minutes of being in Year Three."

Ava was trying to imagine what those six hours in Year Three might have been like when there was a pounding on Isabel's door. Then came the five words that, when spoken by younger brothers and sisters, can ruin any play date: "Can we play with you?"

When Isabel tried to hold the door closed, the littlies began shrieking, "Let us in or we'll tell!" The big girls knew they had been beaten. Isabel let go of the door, and Lola and the Reds came tumbling in, with buckets from the garden on their heads and mud on their shoes. Johnny trailed behind them, helping baby Rafe toddle down the hallway.

The little girls swarmed on Isabel's toys. Scarlett and Ruby began rummaging around Isabel's craft table, tossing pens and crayons everywhere. Lola went straight for the fancy dress drawer. She found Isabel's fairy wings and put them on. She flew around the room, still wearing the bucket on her head and screaming at the top of her lungs. Ava thought Lola looked more like an angry wasp than a fairy. She nearly crushed Rafe as he crawled across the floor.

Johnny went and sat quietly near Ava and the conkers.

"What's this?" he asked over the noise. He hadn't seen Isabel's conker collection before. He was holding up a shrivelled conker from a few autumns ago. Isabel had glued cotton wool on its head and made it tiny glasses out of a paperclip.

"It is the grandfather conker," said Ava. "You know conkers? The brown seeds you see everywhere? Isabel makes people out of them."

"Seeds?" asked Johnny. "Can you grow a grandfather?"

Ava laughed. "No, conkers come from horse chestnut trees. So if you put this in the ground,

some day a horse chestnut tree would grow."

"Look what I can do!" shouted Scarlett, looking up from her scribbling. "Watch, super conkers! They can fly!" She snatched a girl conker and a cat conker and tossed them out of the open window.

"Scarlett, nooooooo!" wailed Isabel. They all peered down into the garden, looking for the conker creatures amongst the flowerbeds.

"I'll find them," said Johnny helpfully. He trotted off back downstairs. Ava was thinking they'd got rid of the only littlie that wasn't a maniac. She was sad to see him go.

Little Rafe was sad too. "Oooooohhnnnnnyyy," he screeched, because he wasn't even two yet and he couldn't say Johnny properly. As he turned to follow Johnny, Rafe spotted Zoe upside down on the bed.

"Oooo-eeee," he cried, because he couldn't say Zoe properly either. He tried to stand up to get to his sister faster, but he crashed sideways into the Barbie caravan. No one had time to help him because at that very moment, fairy-wasp Lola launched herself off Isabel's toy chest right on to upside-down Zoe's tummy. Ava was terrified that Zoe's purple head would explode from the attack.

After that there was a lot of crying, then there were a lot of tellings-off by various mummies, and then *finally,* at long last, the littlies were carted off downstairs to watch a bit of TV before going-home time.

Ava, Isabel, Lottie and Zoe (who was right-side up and a nice normal colour again) went back to making a proper plan for the Year Sixes.

"We could just hide from them," said Lottie. "Mrs Peabody could tell everyone to come to school a bit early, and then we could lock the doors before they get there and pretend the school is closed." Ava pictured the Year Sixes with their faces pressed up against the school windows, trying to see if anyone was inside.

"I don't think getting to school earlier is a good idea," said Ava finally. "Mummy and I find it hard enough to get to school on time as it is. Any earlier and we'd still be in our pyjamas."

"Us too," said Isabel. "Maybe we could just ask the Year Sixes nicely to go?"

"Asking nicely never works with eleven-year-olds," said Lottie. Her cousin was eleven so Ava supposed that Lottie knew what she was talking about. Lottie probably had lots of notebook entries about eleven-year-olds.

Lottie must have been thinking about her notebook too, because she suddenly said that she didn't have it. There was a frantic search until Zoe spotted it under some papers on Isabel's craft table.

Lottie seemed very relieved, until she began to look through it. Then she began to scream.

Ava saw that on almost every page, covering entry after entry, were marks of every shape and colour. Most were just scribbles, but there were two wobbly letters that appeared over and over again: R for Ruby, and S for Scarlett.

It took Lottie a long, long time to stop crying. She felt so terrible that she couldn't even bring herself to go downstairs to tell on Ruby and Scarlett.

The four friends sat down on the rug in a circle. Lottie's ruined notebook lay on the floor in the middle, and all around them were piles of fancy dress clothes, crumpled-up sheets of paper and pens without their tops on. Conkers spilled out of the crushed Barbie caravan.

"I want to go home," said Lottie at last.

"Me too," said Zoe. "My tummy hurts."

Isabel looked hurt. She wanted everyone to have fun at her house. But Ava had to agree: this play date had gone horribly wrong. It was a terrible ending to a terrible day.

"I mean, I love coming to your house Isabel," Lottie explained, her eyelashes still wet with tears. "It's just when the littlies are here it is so noisy and crowded and everything gets ruined—"

"Wait a minute," Ava nearly shouted. "That's it!"

"That's what?" said Zoe.

"Lottie loves play dates, but not when they are horrible and awful like this one. If the Year Sixes won't leave Crabtree School because they love it so much," Ava went on, "then we have to make them STOP loving it so much."

"And how do we do that?" asked Isabel crossly, as she tried to put the Barbie caravan back together.

But Lottie had already figured it out. "We make Crabtree School as horrible as this play date!" she shouted. "That's a great idea, Ava!"

It was such a great idea that it made them all feel good enough to go downstairs to tell on Scarlett and Ruby. As they stood up, Isabel said to Ava, "You're lucky, you know. Johnny is not nearly as terrible as the Reds. He's the only littlie that's been good today."

That made Ava worry a little, because things tended to go very wrong when Johnny was trying to be good.

"Where did he go, anyway?" asked Isabel. "Is he still in the garden?"

Apart from feeling bad for Lottie, the mums weren't terribly concerned with what the littlies had got up to. They had finished their one thousand cups of tea and now it was time to go home. When that time comes mums can only think of one thing: getting out the door as soon as possible.

In the flurry of tidying up and searching for

shoes and stuffing the littlies into their coats, the big girls made a plan to save their school. They would need help from Mrs Peabody and all the teachers, but they thought it just might work.

They were nearly finished planning when Lottie's mum interrupted them. "That's funny," she said. "I can't find my car keys. I thought they were in my bag." She had her purse and some work papers and her phone all strewn over the hallway floor. No keys. Lottie's mum went to search in the sitting room.

Zoe's mum couldn't find her car keys, either. Even Isabel's mum's keys were missing off the front table.

"Where is Johnny?" asked Ava's mum suddenly. Her keys were missing too.

They all went out into the garden. Johnny was digging in the flower beds with a small spade.

"I hope he isn't digging up my flowers!" said Isabel's mum.

"I hope he hasn't buried my conkers!" said Isabel.

"Johnny," said his mum. "Everyone seems to be missing their keys. Have you seen any car keys?"

"Yes, Mummy," said Johnny. "I planted them, all around the garden. I'm going to grow us new cars!"

Isabel, Lottie, Zoe and Ava just looked at each other. Play date number ninety-five went on record as the worst, most horrible, terrible, awfully bad play date ever in the history of the world. Even the mummies, who now had no keys to their cars or houses, agreed. But at least it had given Ava and her friends the perfect plan for saving Crabtree School.

Chapter

Ten Ways to Ruin a School

Ava's second day of being stuck somewhere in between Years Two and Three was a busy one. The night before, she and her friends had stayed up late digging for keys in Isabel's garden. It turned out that Johnny was very good at burying things. That morning Ava's eyes were sleepy as she patted Baron Biscuit.

"Morning, Ava!" said Jessica brightly. "Did you miss me yesterday?"

Ava nearly jumped out of her skin. She'd spent so long talking *about* Jessica that she'd forgotten what it was like talking *to* her.

"I did miss you," said Ava. It was the truth. "Are you going to be here every morning from now on?"

"Yes, of course," said Jessica. "Every day, forever!"

"Won't you get bored?" wondered Ava. "You've already done Year Six once."

"Nah," replied Jessica. "I could never be bored here. And there's no school anywhere that could be better than Crabtree School."

"How do you know?" asked Ava.

"I just do," said Jessica. She smiled at Ava and started upstairs. For the first time ever, Ava didn't smile back. Forever and ever of watching Jessica walk up those stairs whilst she had to stay on the ground floor with crying Reception girls was going to be way too long.

Back in the Year Two classroom, Ava told her friends about what Jessica had said. Lottie wasn't surprised. "Eleven-year-olds think they know everything," she said. "Our plan had better work."

With Miss Cheeky's help, Ava and her friends called a big meeting for later that morning. While most of the Crabtree girls watched films in their classrooms, the teachers crowded into Mrs Peabody's office. Colonel Crunch and Mrs Crunch were there too, and Mrs Biro, the school secretary. The headmistress was busy trying to figure out what this was all about.

"A few girls in the Year Two class," began Miss Cheeky. "I mean, the Year Three class. I mean – I mean Ava, Zoe, Isabel and Lottie, have come up with a way to help with our Year Six problem."

"I'm not sure that it is a good idea to ask seven-year-olds to solve this problem," said Mrs Peabody to Miss Cheeky. Mrs Peabody wasn't being unkind. Sometimes grown-ups

just forget how clever seven-year-olds can be.

"Let's just listen to what they suggest," said Miss Moody. Miss Moody knew *exactly* how clever seven-year-olds could be.

"We have heard," began Lottie loudly, "that the Year Six girls don't want to leave because they love our school so much."

All the teachers nodded. They had heard that too.

"So we think," Ava said, "that the only way to get them out is to make the school completely impossible to love."

"How could you not love Crabtree School?" said Mrs Peabody. "They told me they love everything: the building, the food, the teachers, *me*. Especially me." Mrs Peabody smiled at the memory.

"So then we know exactly what to ruin," said Ava.

"Just for a little while," added Isabel quickly.

"We'll just ruin it for long enough to make them want to leave."

The teachers were silent. They seemed to be thinking it over. No one said no.

It was Zoe's turn to talk. "Earlier this morning," she told the teachers, "our class made a list of twenty-five wonderful things about Crabtree School. Even if we just choose the ten top answers and ruin those, we should be able to make the school really quite awful."

Lottie took out her notebook and showed the teachers the list. It was long and it looked very impressive. Lottie passed it around the room.

"This is a lovely list, girls," said Mrs Peabody once she had read it, "but I just wouldn't even know how to begin ruining all these wonderful parts of our school."

"I could take care of ruining the food," said Mrs Crunch helpfully.

Colonel Crunch stood at attention. "And I

can ruin the playground," he said. "I'd be proud to be a part of this mission." He saluted them all.

Soon everyone was talking all at once. Making plans to ruin a perfectly lovely school turned out to be quite fun.

When they had finished their meeting, the teachers sneaked off to tell their classes about the plan. The Year Six teacher, Mrs Swan, went to make sure her class, who were the ones causing all this trouble in the first place, didn't suspect anything. Everyone knew what to do, and in case they got confused, Lottie had written everything down in her notebook, carefully avoiding the scribbled-on pages.

When everyone was gone, Mrs Peabody called Lottie, Isabel, Zoe and Ava over to her desk. "Girls," she said. "I'm so proud of you and your whole class. You've done a brilliant job of planning to destroy our school. Well done!" She gave them each a hug and a biscuit.

"Although, Lottie," Mrs Peabody said, eyeing Lottie's notebook again, "perhaps we should do a bit of handwriting practice on those Ss and Rs?"

Right before the end of the school day, Ava and her friends made a very important visit to the new Reception class in the Rainbow Room. They told them all about the plan to save Crabtree School.

"So if you want to be *properly* in Reception," Ava concluded, "you have to do exactly what I've just told you. You're big, brave Crabtree girls now and we need you to help us. YOU are the most important part of this plan. Do you promise to do your best? I mean, your worst?"

None of the Reception girls were staring at their shoes this time. All eyes were on Ava as the younger girls made their promises.

Chapter

Forever and Ever Is a Long Time

In the history of Crabtree School for Girls, there has never been before and never will be again a day like Ava's third day of nearly being in Year Three. She and her mum got to school early. Colonel Crunch had already been hard at work. There were big piles of dirt on the path up to the school. The windows had been smudged with mud. When Ava stepped into the front hallway it seemed gloomier than usual.

By nine o'clock everything was ready to go.

"Good morning, Jessica!" said Ava as her favourite Year Six girl came through the front door.

"Good morning!" said Jessica happily. Ava felt a little bit guilty for what was about to happen. But it was too late to turn back now.

Jessica reached down to stroke Baron Biscuit. But Baron Biscuit was covered in bubble wrap and yellow CAUTION tape. A sign around his neck read: DO NOT TOUCH.

"What's going on?" asked Jessica.

"Colonel Crunch says Baron Biscuit is too old and fragile to be stroked any more," Ava told her.

"But what will we do for good luck?" asked Jessica.

Jessica was going to need a whole lot more than luck that day. Just then three of the new Reception girls ran up to her.

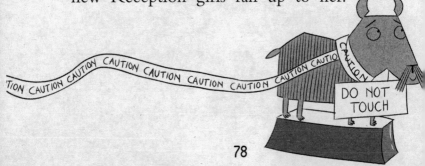

They clung to her dress and shouted, "Play with us, play with us! You be the mummy and we'll be the babies!"

They tugged so hard on Jessica that the skirt ripped off her dress. Then Jessica was standing in the hallway in her pants. The Reception girls ran away laughing, taking the bottom half of Jessica's dress with them. Around the corner, Isabel gave them each a high five as they passed.

"Oh, *Jess*-icaaaa," sang a voice from inside the headmistress's office. "Come here please, my little darling!"

Ava followed Jessica into the office. As usual, Mrs Peabody was wearing one of her lovely flowery dresses, and her candyfloss hair looked especially fluffy. The headmistress smiled a huge smile when they came in.

"Jessica, my love," said Mrs Peabody, giving Jessica a huge hug. "What happened to your uniform dress?" Before Jessica could answer the headmistress gave her another hug and a kiss on each cheek.

"Now, darling." The headmistress squeezed Jessica's face between her hands. "You really must wear a whole dress. I can't have you catching cold now, can I?"

"But Mrs Peabody, someone ripped my dress—" began Jessica.

"You poor thing!" said Mrs Peabody. "How embarrassing! My poor little angel!" And even though Jessica was nearly as tall as the headmistress, Mrs Peabody wrapped her in an old blanket that Lady Lovelypaws sometimes used for a bed. Then she scooped Jessica up like a baby and began to rock her back and forth. It looked so silly that Ava nearly laughed out loud. Jessica was horrified.

"Now we really must get you sorted," said Mrs Peabody. She reached for the lost property box that was just inside her office door. She pulled out a school uniform dress. "This should be perfect," she said to Jessica. "Here you go, poppet."

The dress was way too small. It would have even been too small on Ava, and poor Jessica could hardly breathe it was so tight. But before Jessica could complain Mrs Peabody was digging through the box again. She pulled out a hat, scarf and gloves that someone had lost last winter, and she put them on Jessica. Then she wrapped her up in the blanket again. Ava noticed that it was covered in cat hair.

"There, angel," she said. "You must have been freezing standing there in your pants! These will warm you up!"

It was only early autumn, so Jessica hadn't been cold. And now that she was dressed for winter, she was very, very warm. Ava could see her sweating.

"Hot chocolate, girls?" asked Mrs Peabody. "Biscuits?"

At first that sounded nice. Ava and Jessica both had some chocolate digestives. But then Mrs Peabody insisted that Jessica try some lovely gingerbread men too, and have another hot chocolate. And some chocolate fingers. And another hot chocolate. Then Mrs Peabody just happened to find some other biscuits in her desk, which were lovely and delicious and had cream in the middle so Jessica simply *had* to try those. By her twentieth biscuit, Jessica could hardly chew she was so full, but Mrs Peabody took out a box of Jammie Dodgers and smiled brightly.

Sometimes you can have too much of a nice thing.

By the time Jessica was able to escape Mrs Peabody's office, she hoped she'd never see another biscuit of any kind, ever again. She'd also had enough hugs to last her until she was a hundred years old.

When Jessica was gone Mrs Peabody picked

up a walkie-talkie from her desk. "Operation *Biscuit Tin* is complete," she said over the radio.

"Roger that," said Ava, who had been lurking in the hallway. Colonel Crunch had taught her that "Roger" meant "I understand". Ava pushed another button on the walkie-talkie. "Colonel Crunch, Jessica's heading for the Year Six classroom. The targets are all assembled."

Ava and Zoe sneaked up to the Year Six classroom behind Jessica. They stood in the doorway and peeked in.

The first person they saw was Elizabeth. For once in her life, she wasn't talking. At least not properly.

"Acissej. . ." Elizabeth spluttered. "Erehw evah uoy neeb?" Whatever Elizabeth was trying to say made no sense at all, and it was taking ages for her to get it out.

"Mrs Swan said that since Elizabeth is so

good at talking, for her second time in Year Six she has to learn to say everything backwards!" Ava heard another Year Six girl tell Jessica.

Then Ava spotted Lucy, another of Jessica's classmates. Lucy's sparkly headband had been snapped in two and she was holding a huge chunk of her own hair. "One of the new Reception girls cut it off!" she told Mrs Swan.

Mrs Swan had her feet up on her desk. She was reading a book.

"Oh dear, that's too bad, Lucy," said Mrs Swan, patting her on the head. "Were they playing hairdresser? They're so little they hardly know what they are doing." Mrs Swan wasn't really paying attention. She hadn't even taken the register yet.

"Sorry, girls," continued Mrs Swan. "This book is so good I can't put it down. I'll just finish this chapter whilst you get settled."

The Year Six girls sat down at their desks. They

waited. And waited. The book Mrs Swan was reading must have been very good. Mrs Swan laughed. She cried. She forgot all about her class.

After ages and ages, Mrs Swan finally stood up and wrote something on the white board in very, very tiny letters.

The entire class leaned forward over their desktops to try to read what she had written. Suddenly there was a great creaking noise and all of the Year Six desks collapsed on the floor.

"Whoops-a-daisy!" said Mrs Swan. "I guess you must be getting too big for those desks, girls! Ah well, never mind." She went back to her book.

The Year Six girls sat amongst the broken remains of their desks. Ava watched from the doorway. The screws that normally held the desks together were in Mrs Swan's desk, where Ava had hidden them after school yesterday.

"How did you even think of that?" whispered Zoe.

Ava smiled to herself. Johnny was always taking things apart. He had a whole collection of bolts and screws under his bed. Things came crashing down all the time at Ava's house: cupboards, shelves, doll buggies, dining chairs...

Sometimes little brothers can teach you a thing or two. If they don't crush you first.

"Operation *Screw Loose*, mission

accomplished," said Zoe into the walkie-talkie. "Begin Operation *Peace and Quiet*."

"Roger that," came back Colonel Crunch's voice. Suddenly the loudest noise Ava had ever heard filled the Year Six classroom. Everyone ran to the open window. In the playground below, Colonel Crunch was drilling into a huge piece of metal.

"Apologies!" he screamed over the screeching, grinding, brrruming noise. "I'm making an extension for the slide."

"Close the window!" shouted Jessica. But they couldn't close the window, because it was stuck. It was stuck because Colonel Crunch had superglued it open earlier that morning.

Mrs Swan opened her desk drawer and took out a pair of earmuffs. She put them on and then looked at her class.

"Oh dear, don't you have any earmuffs, girls? Always be prepared, that's what I say!" she shouted over the noise. None of the Year Six girls had any earmuffs. Jessica did have the hat from lost property. She tried to pull it down over her ears but nothing could block the sound of Colonel Crunch's drill.

"Mrs Swan?" screamed Jessica. "What shall we do now?"

Mrs Swan pointed to the tiny letters on the board.

The Year Six girls leaned forward again over the pieces of their desks. The tiny word on the white board read:

NOTHING

"That says nothing," shouted Jessica.

"I wrote the WORD nothing," shouted Mrs Swan. "But actually that word does say *something*. It tells you what we are going to learn today."

"We are going to learn nothing today?" shouted Lucy.

"Exactly!" yelled Mrs Swan. "You already know everything there is to learn in Year Six. So we shall all have to find things to keep ourselves busy! Now if you'll excuse me, girls, this book really is very good."

"But we need something to do!" shouted Jessica.

"OK, fine, girls. If you insist!" yelled Mrs Swan. She stood and wrote on the whiteboard again, in bigger letters:

Please write "WE LOVE CRABTREE SCHOOL
AND WE WANT TO STAY FOR FOREVER
AND EVER" five thousand times.

The Year Six girls couldn't really complain because they'd asked for something to do. It took AGES, and it was much worse than doing nothing. By the time they were done writing, Mrs Swan had finished her book, knitted an entire jumper and was painting her fingernails.

For the Year Sixes, the day only got worse as it went on.

PE was a disaster.

Year Five, who were very cross about not being in Year Six like they were supposed to be, had been more than happy to help with Year Three's plan. They had taken all of the Year Six PE kits and coated the bottoms of their trainers with cooking oil from the kitchen. The Year Sixes slipped and slid through the school as they made their way outside.

"Whatever is the matter with you today, girls?" asked Mrs Yards, the PE teacher.

Mrs Yards made the Year Sixes stand on their heads in the playing field for their entire PE lesson. "This is great for building strong minds!"

she shouted over the noise of Colonel Crunch's drilling. "If you aren't going to Year Seven we have to keep everything you learned in Year Six right at the tippy-top of your brains!" Greasy oil from their shoes dripped down over the Year Six girls' faces.

To make matters worse, when Colonel Crunch finally finished his drilling he decided to water the flowers on the edge of the playing field. But he kept watering the upside-down Year Six girls instead.

"Whoops! Sorry, Miss White!" he said to Jessica. "I thought you were a giant sunflower. I must get new spectacles."

Lottie, Isabel, Zoe and Ava crowded around a window to watch Operation *Slip 'n' Slide*.

"Is it too mean?" asked Ava, as one of the Year Sixes toppled over on to the wet grass.

"No," said Zoe. "It's the only way to get them out. And isn't it funny how red their

faces have gone from being upside down?"

"Yes," said Ava. "They look just like tomatoes."

Ava and her friends all moved away from the window as the freshly watered, tomato-headed Year Sixes came back inside. They slipped past Mrs Peabody's office in their slimy shoes.

"There's so much more good stuff coming up!" said Lottie, looking through her notebook. "Operation *PE* complete," she said into the walkie-talkie. "Begin Operation *Crumble Jumble*, Mrs Crunch."

"Roger," came back Mrs Crunch's voice.

On the way to lunch the Year Sixes passed the Rainbow Room. Isabel and Lottie had been hard at work there all morning. The fairy lights and fuzzy rug were in a sad little pile in the hallway. "Health and Safety," Colonel Crunch told Jessica and her friends as they passed. "If the Rainbow Room is going to be another Reception classroom, we have to make some changes."

That morning the new Reception girls had scribbled all over the walls of the Rainbow Room. With help from Isabel and Lottie, they had torn up the beanbag chairs too, so it looked like it had snowed beans. The Rainbow Room had become the Blizzard Room.

Lunchtime was the most awful thing of all.

Usually there were two lunches, one earlier for the younger half of the school and then a later lunch for the bigger girls. But not today. Mrs Crunch said she was honoured that the Year Six class wanted to stay. She made an important announcement: from now on all of Crabtree School would eat together. The dining room was so crowded that the Year Sixes were forced to eat with the new Reception class on their laps. Ava, Lottie, Zoe and Isabel squeezed right in with the Year Sixes so that they could see their plan at work.

The Reception girls from both this year *and* last year made sure to cry all the time and to spill A LOT. Lunch was a brand new recipe: broccoli, turnip and porridge bake with some strange kind of purple meat in it.

"Kcuy," said Elizabeth, and you didn't need to be good at listening backwards to understand her.

Pudding was Mrs Crunch's apple crumble.

"At least," said Jessica to Elizabeth over the screeching of the Reception girls, "at least it is my favourite pudding today." She took a huge bite of apple crumble.

"And four, three, two, one..." Zoe was whispering to Ava.

"AHHHHHHHHH! YUCK!" Jessica screamed. "IT'S. SO. SOUR!!!" But when she reached for her glass of water, she found bits of broccoli floating in it. The Reception girl in her lap had been washing her hands in Jessica's drink.

"Mrs Crunch, this apple crumble tastes, errr, *different* from usual," said Jessica when she was sure she wasn't going to be sick. Even though she was miserable, Jessica was still trying to be polite. Ava had to admire that.

"New recipe," said Mrs Crunch. "It's *crab* apple crumble. No use wasting all of these

perfectly delicious crab apples, especially when we have extra mouths to feed. Why, just this morning I gathered enough of our crab apples to serve this apple crumble every single day for forever and ever."

"Forever and ever is a long time," said Jessica softly.

"It is indeed," said Mrs Crunch.

Chapter

There's Nothing Worse than a Nice Headmistress

The messiest, loudest, slipperiest, most confusing, wettest, worst-tasting day ever at Crabtree School was drawing to a close. It was nearly time to go home, and all Ava could do was hope that their plan had been enough to ruin the best school in the world.

Zoe had been sure that the Year Sixes would run off screaming straight away after lunch, but she was wrong. Ava could see that both of Zoe's watches now said three p.m., and Jessica and her classmates were all still there. They looked terrible though: the Year Sixes were exhausted, starving and covered in mess. They were wandering from room to room like lost puppies. The rest of the Crabtree girls were tired and hungry too, and the Reception girls both new and old had sore throats from screaming so much.

It was time for Jessica, Elizabeth and the rest of their class to decide whether they could face another day at the new and different Crabtree School. Moving on had to be *their* idea. This was important because, according to Lottie, eleven-year-olds did not like being told what to do. But none of these eleven-year-olds looked well enough to decide anything, so Mrs Peabody called Jessica and Elizabeth into her office to see if she could give them a little nudge in the right direction.

Ava and Zoe rushed back to their old hiding place under the crab apple trees, bringing Isabel along with them. Lottie was nowhere to be found. Today Mrs Peabody's window was open just a crack, and they could hear everything that was happening in her office.

"So," said Mrs Peabody. "Are you still planning to stay with us for forever and ever?" The headmistress gave Jessica and Elizabeth a huge smile and pulled out a tray of biscuits. Jessica looked as if she'd just been offered a plate of big hairy spiders.

"Yes," said Jessica quietly. She was tugging at the very, very small uniform dress Mrs Peabody had given her that morning. It was so tight that the sleeves were pinching her arms.

"Yes, what?" asked Mrs Peabody, looking extremely puzzled.

"Yes, we still want to stay," said Jessica. Elizabeth just nodded. She'd had just about enough of talking for one day.

"For forever and ever?" gasped Mrs Peabody. "Still?"

103

"Yes," said Jessica.

"Sey," said Elizabeth firmly.

"Are you telling me that you like the changes we've made around here?" said Mrs Peabody. "And you won't get fed up of having lunch with four-year-olds every single day?"

"Well, I don't like crab apple crumble," admitted Jessica, who even then couldn't quite get the sour taste out of her mouth. "But this is my school and I still love it."

"Me too," said Elizabeth. "I mean, em oot."

"Oh, girls," said Mrs Peabody. She didn't know whether to be *pretend* kind, which wasn't really kind at all, or *genuinely* kind, like she usually was.

Ava and her friends looked at each other. They couldn't think of anything to do. It was all up to Mrs Peabody now.

"Girls," she said gently, "if you really feel you need to, maybe you can stay a bit longer."

She didn't squish their cheeks or give them any fake hugs.

"She's ruining it!" whispered Zoe.

Suddenly there was a loud bang. The big bottom drawer of Mrs Peabody's desk slammed open, and a voice coming from inside shouted, "NOOOOOO! This is not what is supposed to happen!"

The sight of Lottie popping up from Mrs Peabody's drawer startled Isabel so much that she fell back against a crab apple tree. Dozens of crab apples showered down on Ava and Zoe. Both of them shouted.

Everyone inside the office heard them, but no one cared. They were watching Lottie, who was very, very cross and stamping her feet on the bottom of the desk drawer. Mrs Peabody's desk was tipping dangerously to and fro.

"How can you possibly, possibly, ever want to stay ONE MORE SINGLE MINUTE at

Crabtree School?" screeched Lottie. "We've worked so hard! Everything was so perfectly, wonderfully awful!"

"You mean you did it on purpose?" asked Jessica. She looked at Mrs Peabody and Lottie, then out of the window at Ava. "The noise, the food, the standing on our heads? You want us to leave that much?" Her feelings were hurt.

Ava pulled the window open further and stuck her head through so she could see Jessica better. "No. I mean, yes," said Ava. "Yes and no."

"Pardon?" said Jessica.

"I mean, no, we don't want you to leave, because we like you," Ava explained. "But yes, your class has to go. You can't stay in Year Six forever and we DEFINITELY can't stay in Year Two forever."

"Why should we go?" Elizabeth said. She'd had quite enough of speaking backwards. "We've been here for seven years. This is our school!"

"But you're big girls, you don't belong here any more!" cried Zoe.

"I don't understand," said Lottie, who had calmed down a little bit but was still standing in Mrs Peabody's desk drawer. "Yes, it's lovely here. Yes, Crabtree School is the best primary school in the whole world. But just think about all of the amazing things there are about senior school!"

"I don't want to think about it!" shouted Elizabeth. She had found her voice again and there was no going back. "And I won't, I won't, I won't! Never, never, never!" She sounded like one of Isabel's little sisters. She was even stamping her feet.

Then Ava heard the sound of someone sniffling. Jessica had tears running down her cheeks. Mrs Peabody's hands began to shake and her eyes got googly. Even Ava had to admit that it was terrible to see an eleven-year-old crying in school. What was going on here? Jessica and Elizabeth were acting just like the new Reception girls.

And then all of the sudden Ava understood: The Year Six girls were *scared*.

Crabtree School was the cosiest, warmest, safest school on Earth. And even on its very worst day, it wasn't the kind of place that was easy to leave behind.

Chapter

Actually, Lunch Is the Most Important Meal of the Day

Outside Mrs Peabody's window a small crowd had gathered behind Ava and her friends. Colonel and Mrs Crunch were there, and so were Mrs Swan and Miss Cheeky and Mrs Yards. There were also a few stray Reception girls who had been following Ava around all day. Everyone had been watching, and now everyone seemed to understand that a new plan was needed.

Mrs Peabody calmed herself down and crouched beside Jessica and Elizabeth. She did her best not to look at Jessica's tears.

110

"Girls," she said. "I know it is a bit scary, but think of all the wonderful new friends you'll make, and the lovely things you'll learn at your new schools."

Mrs Peabody sounded exactly like what she was: a grown-up trying to make children feel better. It didn't work.

The trouble was that Mrs Peabody really didn't know anything about Year Seven. It had been a *very* long time since she was eleven. Her job as headmistress of a primary school meant that what she did know about school ended in Year Six.

Ava didn't know much about Year Seven either, but whatever they had there must be *even* better than your own proper desk and overnight camping trips. There had to be *something* that would make these Year Six girls want to move up.

"Lottie," said Ava. "Is there anything in your notebook about Year Seven?"

Lottie took her notebook out of her pocket. She flipped through the pages. Her cousin was going into Year Seven, and she'd written something about it in there somewhere. But it was hard to read anything because of all the scribbles.

Ava tried to think of the most grown-up thing possible. Doing things on your own is very grown-up.

"Maybe in Year Seven, you can walk to school all by yourself," she said to Jessica. "Without your mum!"

Jessica had stopped crying. "I already do that," she told Ava. "I have done since Year Five."

Year Five was only two years on from Year Three. Suddenly Ava wasn't sure she liked the sound of walking to school all by yourself. It sounded scary. And lonely.

"Lunch," muttered Lottie, still looking through her notebook. "It was something to do with lunch in Year Seven."

"Girls," said Mrs Peabody to Jessica and Elizabeth. "You see, you're *already* so grown-up. And despite Elizabeth's best efforts, going backwards doesn't work: I think Jessica found out this morning that being a baby is no fun!"

Jessica nodded in agreement. It wasn't fun.

"Onwards!" Colonel Crunch shouted from outside the window. "You have to keep marching on, girls. You can't stay in one place forever!"

There was silence in the office. Jessica and Elizabeth were thinking. The only sound was Lottie turning the pages of her notebook.

"I found it!!!" shrieked Lottie. "My cousin says that in Year Seven, after lunch you are allowed to do WHATEVER YOU WANT during break time."

Elizabeth and Jessica already knew that. But there was more.

Lottie drew a huge breath. "AND THEN,"

she said dramatically, "when you get to Year Twelve, you can even go out to a café for lunch. BY YOURSELF. WITHOUT ANY GROWN-UPS."

Lunch with your friends sounded much better to Ava than walking to school all alone. You could walk to the café together. You could have a table to yourself, and order chocolate cake and chips followed by apple crumble for pudding. You could have secret meetings and plan sleepovers and... Ava was daydreaming. And she was doing it out loud: everyone in the office was listening to her.

After a short while, Ava remembered that she was standing in the window of the headmistress's office and not in a café. She stopped talking. But looking around, she saw that she was not the only one daydreaming. Jessica and Elizabeth were too. For the first time, they were picturing something beyond Crabtree School.

The best part was that this daydream could become true life, if they were brave enough to let it.

Jessica and Elizabeth looked at each other the way that best friends do when they need to talk without words. Without having to say anything, they came to a decision. They had got past even the most grown-up things that a seven-year-old can think of, and it was time to find out what else was out there.

When they agreed to go, Mrs Peabody said that she was very proud of them all, and offered everyone a biscuit. The headmistress had tears in her eyes, and Ava wondered if her own tears would make Mrs Peabody's eyes *extra* googly and her hair stand up and maybe even her head spin round. Lady Lovelypaws seemed worried about this as well and rubbed up against Mrs Peabody's legs to calm her down. Then Lady Lovelypaws rubbed up against Elizabeth and Jessica's legs too, as if she were saying goodbye.

"Ava," said Jessica before she left Mrs Peabody's office, "maybe some days I can meet you by the gate after school and walk you home. I'll get my mum to ask your mum."

Ava couldn't think of anything she'd like more. She leaned in through the window to give Jessica a hug. When Jessica raised her arms to hug Ava back, there was a loud tearing sound as the back of the lost property uniform dress ripped open at the seams. The Year Sixes had well and truly outgrown Crabtree School.

Chapter

Year Three, Really and for Real

It was quite easy for Jessica and Elizabeth to convince the rest of their class that it was time to leave Crabtree School. Zoe thought it was the bit about having lunch without grown-ups that had done it. Lottie said it was because eleven-year-olds always wanted to do whatever their friends did. Probably they were both right.

Colonel Crunch had given the Year Six girls a final salute as they marched out of the school gates. They promised to come and visit often and to bring back news of Year Seven.

By just after nine o'clock the next morning, Crabtree School was almost back to normal. The front windows were shiny and sparkling and Baron Biscuit was strokeable again. Mrs Peabody was in her office having hot chocolate and biscuits with Lady Lovelypaws, who now had a new bed made of bubble wrap. Colonel Crunch was busy hanging the fairy lights back up in the Rainbow Room. There were delicious smells coming from the kitchen.

The new Reception girls were happily settled into their proper Reception classroom. They were making collages out of the extra beans from the beanbag chairs. Not a single one of them was crying.

Ava was once again at her desk in the Year Three classroom, looking out over the park. She was thinking about the big girls in Year Seven, and about what secondary school must be like. Wouldn't it be brilliant to walk across

the park to a café? Or maybe not a café. Maybe a fancy restaurant, like the one her mum and dad went to for their anniversary. Zoe, Isabel and Lottie could come too. They could all wear high heels and lipstick with their uniforms. Or maybe they could bring fancy dresses to change into. And they could have perfume. Grown-up ladies always wore perfume when they went out to dinner. They could all sit at a big table with fancy plates and lots of crystal glasses for clinking, and maybe there would be music and dancing, maybe some violins or a piano and ice creams with loads of cherries on top.

"Ava," said Miss Moody. The whole class was staring at Ava. "Ava, are you here with us this morning? We are in Year Three at Crabtree School, where might you be?"

"Sorry, Miss Moody," said Ava. "I'm here now!" She turned her attention back to her teacher. Year Three began again, really and for real this time, and Ava knew that she was exactly where she belonged.

Turn the page
for lots more
Crabtree School
fun!

TWENTY-FIVE THINGS WE LOVE ABOUT CRABTREE SCHOOL
BY YEAR THREE (NOT TWO!!!!)

1) Mrs Crunch's Apple Crumble
2) Watching films and eating popcorn in the Rainbow Room
3) Baron Biscuit
4) Lady Lovelypaws
5) Hot chocolate and biscuits with Mrs Peabody
6) Face-painting at the School Summer Fair
7) Miss Cheeky
8) Extra-cheesy pizza lunches on Friday
9) PE lessons with Mrs Yards, esp. dancing!!!
10) Music lessons with Mr Rockanroll
11) Father Christmas visiting in December
12) The smell of the roses that grow along the back fence in the playground

13) The squishy clay in the art room
14) All-school teddy bear picnics in Crabtree Park
15) Pretending to ice-skate on the floor in the school foyer
16) Colonel Crunch teaching chess on the giant chessboard in the playground
17) The all-school Halloween parade
18) Mrs Peabody
19) Class trips to ice-skate on the pond in Crabtree Park
20) The gazillions of books in the school library
21) The Crabtree School tree house
22) Sports Day
23) The caterpillar house in the playground
24) The Spring Pet Parade
25) The last day of school running-through-the-sprinklers party

ALL ABOUT ME

MY FULL NAME: Ava Alexandra Hughes.

WHERE I LIVE: 77 Crabtree Lane. My house is probably haunted!! There are fairies in the garden too.

WHAT MY ROOM LOOKS LIKE: My room is in the tower at the top of our house! It is pink and has a big doll's house.

WHO IS IN MY FAMILY: Mummy, Daddy and my brother, Johnny.

MY PETS: I have a cat called Marden. He looks like an alien.

MY BEST FRIEND(S): Zoe, Lottie and Isabel.

WHAT I LOVE TO DO: Make up stories, play dressing up, hunt for fairies in the garden.

WHAT MAKES ME CROSS: When people tell me to stop daydreaming!!!

WHAT I AM MOST AFRAID OF: The dark.

WHAT I COLLECT: Snow globes.

MY SECRET HIDING PLACE: I have two!!! The secret drawer in the top of my dresser, and a little hole in a tree in the garden.

ALL ABOUT ME

MY FULL NAME:

WHERE I LIVE:

WHAT MY ROOM LOOKS LIKE:

WHO IS IN MY FAMILY:

MY PETS:

MY BEST FRIEND(S):

WHAT I LOVE TO DO:

WHAT MAKES ME CROSS:

WHAT I AM MOST AFRAID OF:

WHAT I COLLECT:

MY SECRET HIDING PLACE:

LOTTIE'S JOURNAL - KEEP OUT!!

PLAY DATE NUMBER: 95

SLEEPOVER??? (TICK ONE)

YES   NO ✓

WHOSE HOUSE? Isabel's House

WHO CAME?

Lottie

Ava

Isabel

Zoe

BROTHERS AND SISTERS?

Johnny

Rafe

Scarlett

Ruby

Lola

WAAAAAYYYY TOO MANY!

DID THEY BOTHER US? (TICK ONE)
YES ✓✓✓✓ NO

TREATS WE HAD TO EAT:
NONE 😞

WHAT WE PLAYED:
No playing!!!! Made plan to save Crabtree School
from Year Sixes!
Then dug in garden for 10,000 hours.

LEVEL OF FUN (CIRCLE ONE):
MOST FUN EVER   REALLY FUN   QUITE FUN
NOT FUN   (WORST PLAY DATE EVER)

OTHER THINGS TO REMEMBER ABOUT
THIS PLAY DATE:
Never let the Reds near my notebook!!!!!
They are EVIL!!!!!!!!!!!!!!!!

NOW IT'S YOUR TURN!

PLAY DATE NUMBER:

SLEEPOVER??? (TICK ONE)
YES   NO

WHOSE HOUSE?

WHO CAME?

BROTHERS AND SISTERS?

DID THEY BOTHER US? (TICK ONE)
YES   NO

TREATS WE HAD TO EAT:

WHAT WE PLAYED:

LEVEL OF FUN (CIRCLE ONE):
MOST FUN EVER   REALLY FUN   QUITE FUN
NOT FUN   WORST PLAY DATE EVER

OTHER THINGS TO REMEMBER ABOUT
THIS PLAY DATE:

MRS PEABODY LOVES TO HAND OUT BISCUITS TO THE CRABTREE GIRLS. WHICH TYPE OF BISCUIT ARE YOU? TAKE THE QUIZ TO FIND OUT!

1. What's your favourite subject at school?
a. Maths (like Zoe!)
b. Music
c. PE
d. Humanities

2. What would you most like to do on a play date?
a. Play make-believe
b. Put on a play
c. Play hide-and-seek
d. Make something crafty (Isabel would choose this answer!)

3. What's your favourite pet?
a. Cat (maybe a white fluffy one, like

Lady Lovelypaws?)

b. Hamster

c. Dog (a real one, not a statue like Baron Biscuit!)

d. Rabbit (Isabel has three of these!)

4. Which magical creature would you most like to meet?

a. Unicorn

b. Mermaid

c. Elf

d. Fairy (Ava would choose this answer!)

5. What would your dream holiday be?

a. Camping

b. Disney World

c. Adventure holiday

d. Tropical island with a sandy beach

6. What's the most fun thing about a sleepover?

a. Making a den for all the sleeping bags

b. Midnight feasts

c. Staying up late

d. Telling stories and sharing secrets

7. What's your favourite colour?

a. Red

b. Pink

c. Blue

d. Green

8. What word best describes you?

a. Curious (Lottie would choose this answer, because she is so nosy!)

b. Fun

c. Energetic

d. Dreamer (Ava would choose this answer!)

9. What's your favourite food?

a. Chocolate

b. Burger (Zoe would choose this answer! You can read all about Zoe in Book 2!)

c. Pizza

d. Crisps

Mostly As:
You're a piece of shortbread

You love solving puzzles and you love learning new things – you're first to put your hands up in class, and you often help friends when they have problems. You also really love animals and if you don't have a family pet, you really want one!

Mostly Bs:
You're a party ring

You're the life of the party! You find it really easy to make friends and you want to have as much fun as possible. You love dressing up – the more colours the better! You're always the first person to come up with a new game or an exciting adventure.

Mostly Cs:
You're a chocolate chip cookie

You're a real-life adventurer. You love sports and running around, and one day you'd love to be a famous explorer or an Olympic athlete. You have so many after-school activities to fit in, but you always manage to see your friends too.

Mostly Ds:
You're a pink wafer biscuit

You love daydreaming and imagining yourself in all sort of wonderful fairylands and magical adventures. You love making up stories and playing make-believe games, and you love drawing and painting and making things. Sometimes you're shy but you love your best friends.

CRABTREE SCHOOL

Collect all the Crabtree School books!

Lauren Pearson

CRABTREE SCHOOL

Year Two
Forever and Ever

Lauren Pearson

CRABTREE SCHOOL

Best Friends
for Never

Lauren Pearson

CRABTREE SCHOOL

The Girl Who
Stole the World

Lauren Pearson

CRABTREE SCHOOL

The Case of
the Missing Cat

www.crabtreeschool.com

Win a family set of scooters!

To celebrate the brilliant Crabtree School series we've got four brand new Micro Scooters® to give away! The lucky winner will also receive a signed set of four Crabtree School books.

Scooting as a family is the perfect way to spend quality time together; you can travel in style and then snuggle down at story time with the Crabtree School gang. Ideal for lots of family fun, you won't want to miss out on this amazing prize!

Visit **www.crabtreeschool.com** to enter the free competition before it closes at midnight on 31st December 2015.

Good luck!

*T&Cs apply – visit **www.crabtreeschool.com** for full details

www.micro-scooters.co.uk